It Rained on the Desert Today

written by Ken and Debby Buchanan

illustrated by Libba Tracy

Northland Publishing
A Justin Company

FIRST EDITION

ISBN 0-87358-575-5
Library of Congress Catalog Card Number 93-44813

Cover design by Trina Stahl
Designed by Rudy J. Ramos
Edited by Erin Murphy

Manufactured in Hong Kong by Wing King Tong

0465/5M/4-94

To Kassie and Irv for bestowing a lifetime of love on a little "Dibby Dab," and for their precious gift of water to our desert home.

—D.B. & K.B.

To the grand birth of new seasons.

—L.T.

A sudden wind rattles the windows,
catching me by surprise.
Holding my breath,
I pull back the curtains
and gaze into the sky.

Is it getting darker outside?

Are storm clouds crowding
to darken the day?

Is it finally here?

I wish my heart
would stop pounding so.

I hold my mouth open,
just a little
like my father taught me,
so that I might hear better.

There
in the distance
is a low, rumbling sound. . . .

Is that lightning's voice
I hear?

Yes!

It is!

It's thunder,
singing the good news:

"Rain will visit the desert
today!"

Today we will honor
the monsoon's return
after what seems like
an endless march of
scorching days.

I race to the front porch
to watch the storm's arrival.

As I stand looking out,
I can see my neighbors gathering . . .

old people,
young people,
big people,
little people.

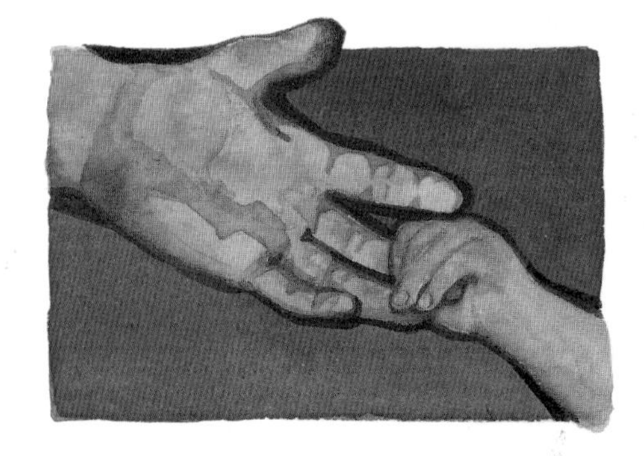

They all wear smiles,
and laughter dances about their faces.

Once together,
we reach for each other's hands
and wait, eagerly,
for the storm to begin.

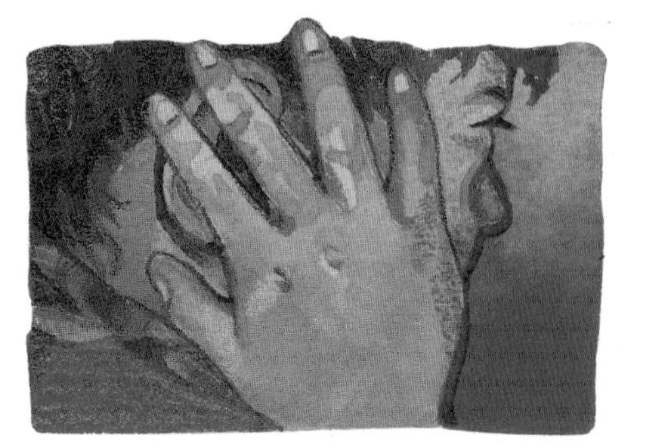

A blinding flash
and a thunderous crash
startle even the bravest
among us!

Our hearts pound in our chests
as the booming echoes roll
across the clouds.

My mouth goes dry
and the hair on my arms
stands up straight
toward the sky.

The rain starts slowly,
with giant water drops
raising small clouds of dust
in the yard.

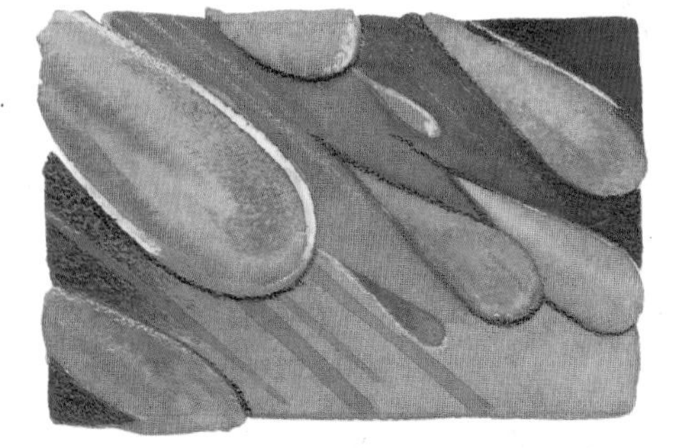

Then Mother Earth sighs
with a huge gust of wind,
and the bottom falls out
of the clouds!

The rain has finally arrived!

It brings thunder and lightning,
crashing and flashing!

They come so loud
it sets my bones to shaking;
so thick,
the desert turns fuzzy gray
and disappears.

Flashes of lightning
brighten each smiling face
as we lift our voices in thanks
for rain, the giver of life.

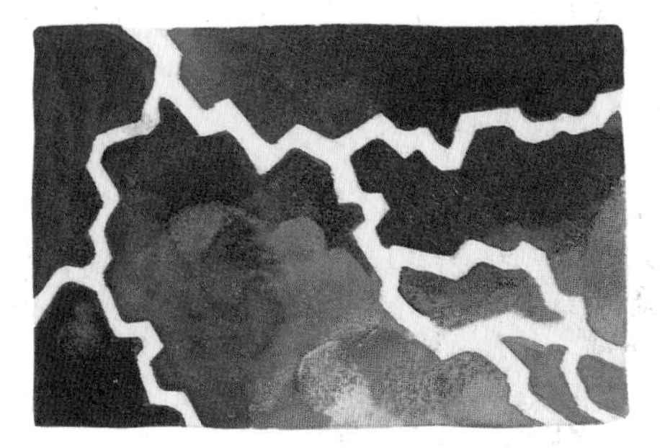

As our voices melt together,
I cannot tell the difference
between the music of the rain
and the voices around me.

Time drifts by
and the rain slowly lessens.

Soon our voices grow still,
and the desert reappears,
as if by magic.

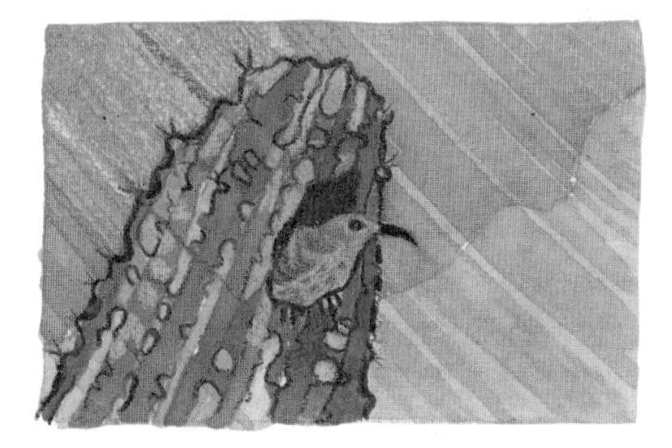

The smaller children
charge into the muddy yard,
dancing in the now gentle rain . . .

slipping and sliding,
falling and rising
and falling back down again,
with laughter for their song.

Then someone says
they look like mud babies
born from the earth herself,
and we all laugh
because we know it's true.

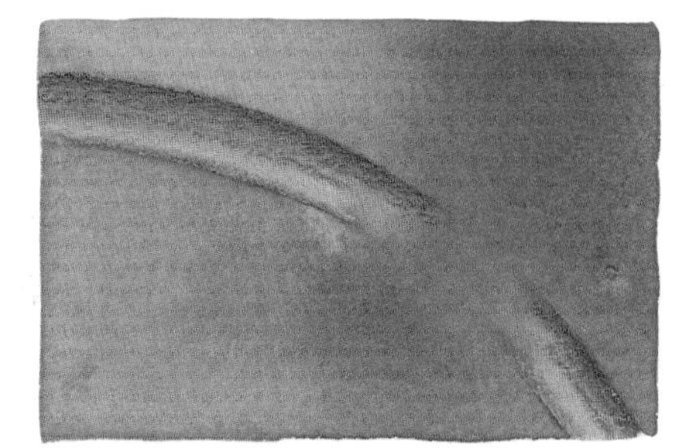

As the rain slows
to a soft, steady rhythm,
its patter matches my heart
beat for beat.

Finally,
the rain stops.

Brilliant sunshine
breaks loose from the clouds
and slices the sky
with a golden beam of light.

A glorious rainbow
bursts across the eastern skies!

Soon Father Sun silently slips
behind the mountain tops,
and the horizon and the sky
are painted with the blazing fire colors
only he knows how to mix.

We each breathe deeply
of the rich desert scents
that ride on the wings
of the damp, gentle wind.

As darkness creeps over the land,
thousands of insects
start weaving their songs
into the distant thunder,
followed by the croaking melodies
of summer's first rain toads
emerging from the mud.

One by one, the children
are thus lullabied to sleep.
Washed clean by the rain,
they are toweled dry,
bundled with care,
and carried home
to their soft, cozy beds
to dream their enchanted dreams.

As the moon starts its climb
across the starlit sky,
I slip into my own bed . . .

and just before sleep comes
to carry me away,
I say a little prayer
of thanks

for the rain

on the desert

today.

Ken Buchanan and his wife, Debby, who grew up in Tucson and have known they were writers since their early days, were inspired after *This House Is Made of Mud* not only to build an adobe home but to co-author children's books. Their first was *Lizards on the Wall; It Rained on the Desert Today* is their second. Writing is something they have to do, says Debby, the way some people have to dance or sing or paint. The Buchanans live in their house made of mud in Arivaca, Arizona, with their two sons and an assortment of pets and wild desert creatures, all of whom celebrate the season's first rain.

Tom Loomis

Craig Wells

Libba Tracy is one of those people who has to paint. She lives with her husband, Tom, and their children near Phoenix, Arizona; while working on the illustrations for *It Rained on the Desert Today,* Libba was also busy carrying her second child, Savannah. Her first, Guy, was produced while she illustrated *This House Is Made of Mud.* Libba's studio looks out upon the Squaw Peak Preserve, and it is from these mountains that her inspiration comes. Originally from South Carolina, Libba adjusted to waiting for summer rain in the Southwest, but still feels reverence when those first summer drops splash down.